Other Black Bear Sled Dog Adventures....

**Black Bear Goes
to Washington**

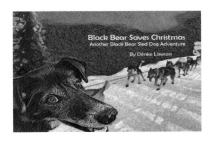

**Black Bear Saves
Christmas**

*What is
Black Bear's next
adventure?*

blackbearsleddog.com

What do sled dogs do when they can no longer pull a sled? Follow Black Bear on her journeys of discovery in the Black Bear Sled Dog book series. This book series helps support retired Alaskan sled dogs.
Visit www.blackbearsleddog.com to learn more about Black Bear and find out about upcoming books.

"*Black Bear Goes to Washington* is unreservedly recommended for family, elementary school, and community library Pets/Wildlife picture book collections."
- Midwest Book Review: Children's Bookwatch (March 2019)

Dedicated to retired sled dogs everywhere.

First Edition

ISBN 978-1-7322303-2-3

Library of Congress Control Number: 2019902059
Printed in the United States of America

Published by Brown & Lowe Books
Springfield, VA
www.brownlowebooks.com

Black Bear Goes to San Francisco

To Maya,
Enjoy your next
adventure!
From,
Black Bear
ogo

Written and Illustrated by
Denise Lawson

D.A. Lawson

Acknowledgements

Thank you Gordon for all you do for Black Bear and her retired friends. Couldn't have done this without you. — D.A.L.

So many cities with so much to see,
My next stop San Francisco... come follow me.

A grizzly named Monarch
on the flag of the state.
Imagine a bear
crossing the Golden Gate!

Sailing past Alcatraz
towards Pier 39,
I saw something in the water,
or was it all in my mind?

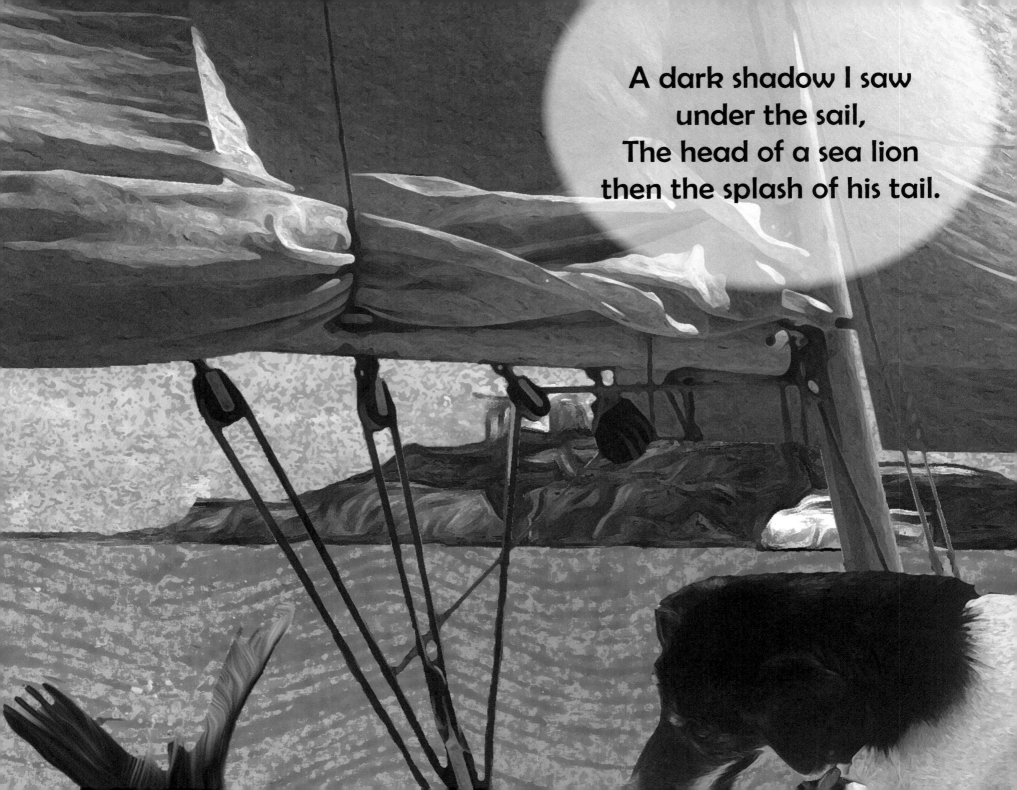

California,
in times of old,
Was the place to go
to prospect for gold.

Alaska offered
another gold rush,
and the Yukon River was
a great place to mush.

Colorful kites seem
to dance on the breeze.
I want to fly one!
Can I try, please?

A crooked street
turning left, turning right,
With traffic and people
all day and all night.

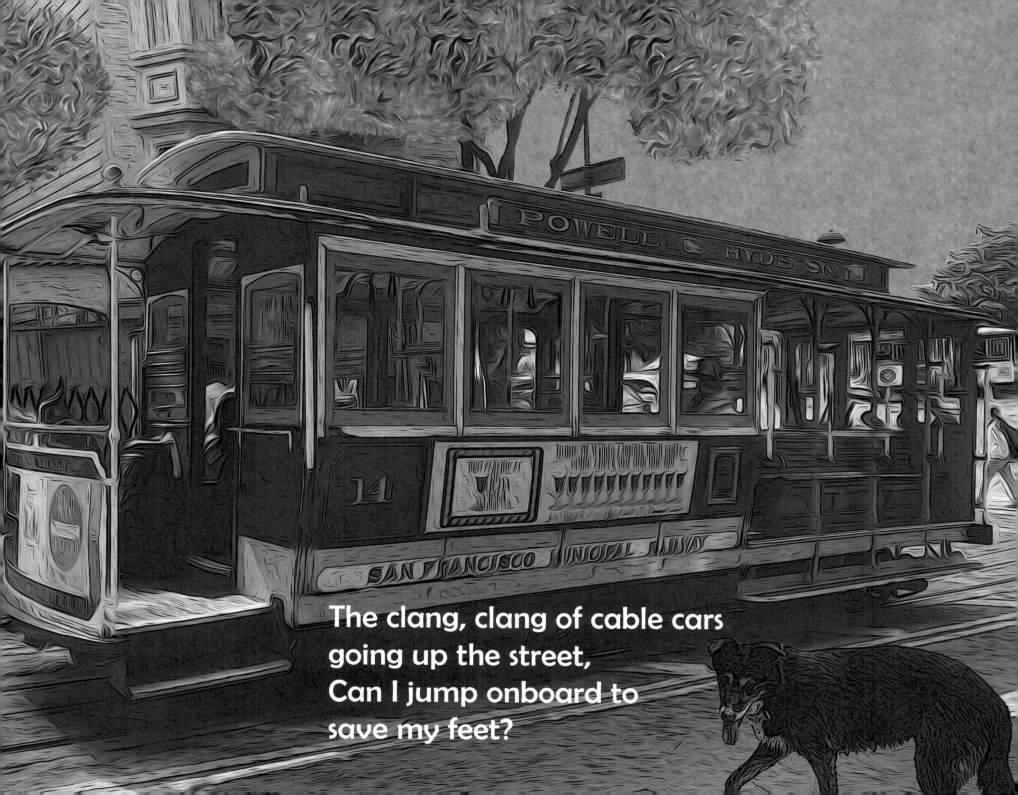

The clang, clang of cable cars
going up the street,
Can I jump onboard to
save my feet?

Never-ending hills climb up and slope down, through the heart of the city and Chinatown.

Lanterns dangle
above my head,
and fill the sky
with balls of red.

As the sun sets,
the lanterns glow.
He said, "Just wait here
for an amazing show."

A dragon parade
passes by,
While sounds of firecrackers
fill the night sky.

A forest of towering trees
so **tall**,
Made me feel
so incredibly small.

Where I lived in Alaska,
I never saw the sea.
Waves crashing on the shore,
so new to me.

I am a sled dog.
I was born to run.
The seals...well, they
think swimming's more fun.

I asked them if
they wanted to play.
"Not now," they said.
"We are on our way!"

North to Alaska,
the place for fish,
Enough to fulfill
every seal's wish.

Nala and Lefty,
Hippo and Dot,
My friends in Alaska,
I miss them a lot.

Black Bear's Guide to Dog Sledding

The musher is the person who drives the sled and gives the commands. Each musher is responsible for the entire dog team. The musher knows the needs and abilities of each dog. Over the years, my mushers always took great care of me. They made sure I had enough food, water, and rest, and they always paid close attention to my feet so I didn't have injuries.

For everyday working, a team doesn't have a set number of dogs. The musher needs to know the weight of the sled and its contents (including the musher) to decide how many dogs are needed on the team. Races, however, have rules about the number of dogs that must start and finish the race. The experience of the musher also determines the number of dogs. The more dogs on the team, the faster the sled will go, so a beginner might start with as few as four dogs.

Lead dogs are at the front of the team and set the pace for the rest of the team. They also need to closely follow the musher's commands and help the musher look out for obstacles that the musher might not be able to see. When I was young, I ran as a lead dog in the famous 1,000-mile Yukon Quest sled dog race. I liked being a lead dog because I could see everything in front of me without other dogs blocking my view.

Swing dogs are right behind the lead dogs. They help the sled turn around corners. Swing dogs are sometimes lead dogs in training. Before I became a lead dog, I was a swing dog and learned by watching the dogs in front of me. I was lucky to learn from other dogs and mushers who were Yukon Quest veterans.

Team dogs run behind the swing dogs. In a large dog team, these dogs would make up most of the team. Dogs don't always stay in the same position. I trust my musher to know when to rotate dogs to different positions.

Wheel dogs are the dogs closest to the sled. They are usually the strongest dogs since they have to pull the most weight.

In dog sledding, we have a lot of ropes called lines that look very confusing, but when the team is all connected, the lines help us pull the sled easily. Each dog has a harness which helps us pull the sled comfortably. In the dog yard, we bark excitedly when we see the musher coming to get us with a harness in hand. Pick me! Pick me! I still have my harness even though I am retired. It still smells like Alaska and brings back great memories.

To be a good member of a dog team, you need to be a good listener especially if you are a lead dog. Here are some commands:
Let's Go – Start running! This is my favorite command because once that harness is on, I can't wait to run!
Gee – Turn right
Haw – Turn left
Easy – Slow down
Whoa! – Stop

Did you know?

The bear on the California state flag was a grizzly named Monarch. Monarch lived in San Francisco. He was the last known wild grizzly in California. The California grizzly is extinct. Alaska still has a lot of grizzly bears.

The gold rush in California came before the gold rush in Alaska. In both places, the gold rush contributed to population growth. The town of Eagle near where I was born was much larger during the gold rush days than it is now. In Alaska, sled dogs helped pull the heavy loads.

Cable cars have a long history in San Francisco. The city has a network of cables that run below the street. The cable cars are pulled by these cables.

The San Francisco Chinese New Year parade is one of the largest outside of Asia. The parade always ends with a dragon dance which is believed to bring good luck. The dragon is so long that it can take 100 or more people to carry it.

Redwood trees grow so well along the California coast because of the climate. Some redwood trees can reach heights of over 350 feet and live for more than a thousand years.

Also by Denise Lawson:

Meet Monique

"Deftly written and charmingly illustrated by Denise Lawson, "Meet Monique" takes children ages 5-8 on a picture book journey as a young girl named Monique looks at an atlas and imagines herself in different places around the world. From the highlands of Scotland to the islands of Trinidad and Tobago, in her imagination Monique plays the bagpipes on a hill full of thistle and plays steel drums barefoot in the sand. On her adventures, she encounters koalas, zebras, and giant pandas and even scales the Eiffel Tower! Thoroughly 'kid friendly' and wonderfully entertaining, "Meet Monique" is especially recommended and unreservedly endorsed for family, elementary school, and community library picture book collections"

Midwest Book Review: Children's Bookwatch (September 2019)

http://www.midwestbookreview.com/cbw/sep_19.htm#Picturebook

CPSIA information can be obtained at www.ICGtesting.com
Printed in the USA
BVIW120459211119
564401BV00004B/4